MW01153488

KIDS ❤ LOVE

TRAVEL MEMORIES!

George & Michele Zavatsky

A Family's Keepsake Book
for Scrapbooking all the
Fun Places You've Visited!

Kids Love Publications

7438 Sawmill Road #500

Columbus, Ohio 43235

www.kidslovepublications.com

Dedicated to the Families
Who <u>Love to Travel!</u>

Be sure to visit our website for our latest creative ideas or for information on our best-selling state travel books:

www.kidslovepublications.com

© Copyright 2001, Kids Love Publications

ISBN# 09663457-6-2

KIDS ♥ TRAVEL MEMORIES ™ Kids Love Publications

BUT WHY THIS BOOK ... AND WHAT'S SO UNIQUE ABOUT IT?

At first glance...you may be asking yourself this question. What makes this book so unique and why is it the best way to remember fun places that you have visited...or are about to visit?

We as a family are thankful to be called "the family that goes on vacation for a living". Over the past several years, we have researched and published several best-selling state travel books. To accomplish this we spent thousands of hours in research, travel, and writing to produce a book that we would be proud to use.

As we promoted our books, we met thousands of people who have the same great thrill that we have, planning the next big adventure, watching the eyes of your kids, and talking about all of the fun times. We encouraged a travel journal and scrapbook to remember those fun times, but had many questions about how to go about assembling these journeys into a timeless, useful way to remember them.

We have compiled in this book, what we believe to be the best of the best...thoughts to remember, ways to remember them, and artwork and graphics that trigger the memories of the special places in your family's history book!

This can be a fun book to use on your journeys, or to assemble in the off season as a family around the kitchen table. What becomes of this book is what you put into it. It is your special family creation that can only be written by those who care to invest in the life of a child.

As children, we were blessed to travel to nearly all 50 states with our family. Over 30 years later, looking at our travel journals, scrapbooks, and souvenirs, we find something very interesting in common. Many times, some of our fondest memories were not made at an expensive attraction, but rather when it was least expected.

Our ultimate mission statement is...that your children will develop a love and a passion for quality family travel experiences that they can pass to another generation of family travelers. We thank you for purchasing this book, and we hope to see you on the road (*and hearing your travel stories!*) God bless your journeys and happy exploring!

George, Michele, Jenny & Daniel

HOW TO USE THIS BOOK
& Tips for Successful Scrapbooking

Here are just a few tips from us to get you started on the fun family project of writing and assembling your new book. But remember, this is your family travel scrapbook - we've only tried to get your thoughts and ideas going...so there's lots of room for creativity!

- Be sure to use "acid-free" calligraphy pens, markers, and glue when adding to your book. This is necessary to prevent future damage to your photographs. Use plastic covers (available from craft or scrapbook supply stores) when you display tickets, brochures, or paper souvenirs that may not be printed on acid-free paper. This book has also been printed on acid-free paper for archival protection.

- Cut or "Crop" pictures to show just the stuff that is important for remembering the place or event. Eliminate any unnecessary or distracting backgrounds. Caution...create a file for negatives or digital images before cutting your original photo!

- Decorate (with your kids' help) the suggested picture frames and crop photos to fit inside them. You may want to use the caption bubbles and frames found on the back of the book's cut-out pages. Or, be really brave and make you own frame with colored paper and paste over.

- The last page of each section in this book is designed for coloring the graphics and/or pasting any additional photos or souvenirs over them.

Happy Scrapbooking!

TABLE OF CONTENTS

Amusements

See a movie 6 stories tall! Ride an old-fashioned antique carousel. Slide down some of the highest coasters. Get lost in a maze. Swing into themed miniature golf parks, Visit a roaring prehistoric forest or "freaky" mystery spot. Or, hang out in the Old West or a wigwam...

The best amusement activity as a family was..._____

_____

_____

The most expensive amusement park was..._____

_____

Mom & Dad's wallet liked this amusement the best..._____

_____

Voted the biggest "tourist trap" and we sure fell in..._____

_____

_____

Biggest "thrill ride" (maybe the tallest coaster or waterslide)..._____

_____

Theme parks where we really felt like we went "back in time"...What made them so-o-o realistic..._____

_____

_____

2

MAZE CRAZE

3

Remove This Page

(to reduce binding thickness as you add personal photos)

Carefully
cut along
the dotted
line

Use these cutouts to add more fun to your pages!

Animals & Farms

Do you have a would-be pet owner in the family...have they taken a tour of the local shelter? Are there really Little Horses, a famous family of Groundhogs, nice snakes or bees, "pampered" fish, or sharks that can't bite you? Do buffalo still roam? Do wolves still howl at the moon? Where does ketchup, ice cream, clothing, or honey come from? Want to learn how they're made?

Unusual animals we met..._____
_____
_____

The "ugliest" animals we saw (and probably didn't touch!)..._____
_____

Pretty creatures great and small...the Lord God made them all..._____
_____

We tasted different flavors of milk at various farms. Which one made the best ice cream?_____
_____
_____

This farm allowed us to actually touch and play with the animals..._____
_____
_____

Remove This Page

(to reduce binding thickness as you add personal photos)

Carefully cut along the dotted line

Use these cutouts to add more fun to your pages!

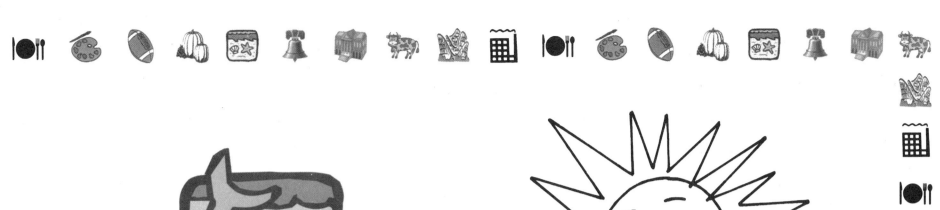

8

History

Skip stones in a creek near Abe Lincoln's, Thomas Edison's, George Washington's, Daniel Boone's, or Native American's homes. See where state government convenes or watch the action in a real courtroom. Living history comes alive at battlegrounds where the fight for freedom was fought by pilgrims and pioneers. Have you ever actually touched (or even hugged) the "Liberty Bell"? Made butter from cream? Printed your own newspaper? Dipped candles? Wove a basket or rug? Harnessed a horse or "forged" housewares?

Our favorite story of a "hometown hero" was ..._____
_____
_____

Something new we learned while touring a war-struck battlefield..._____
_____

A fancy State Capitol building that we toured..._____
_____

Our favorite nickname for a state and why..._____
_____

We walked part of the trail of this legendary Early American hero..._____
_____

Would you enjoy Early American pioneer daily chores?...Which would you like the least?...Which would you like the best?...(aaahh..to go back to simpler times)...._____
_____
_____

Remove This Page

(to reduce binding thickness as you add personal photos)

Carefully
cut along
the dotted
line

Use these cutouts to add more fun to your pages!

Museums

Discover what made historic politicians, inventors, and artists great by touring their childhood homes. (The hint may be in the things they did during playtime!). Visit museums focusing on everything from Wars, to Music, to Modes of Transportation, to Bottle Cap Collections. Pretend you're a jockey, a bus driver, a pilot, a turtle, a pumping human heart, a conductor, a captain, or a race car driver. Maybe you just want to pretend that you're a miner, a pioneer, or an explorer (hard work!).

We had a great conversation with this local character while touring this small museum..._____
_____
_____

What famous person's childhood home did we visit...What unusual things did we learn about their upbringing..._____
_____
_____

The all out best Children's Museum we found was..._____
_____
_____

We learned many new scientific principles at this museum..._____
_____
_____

The most "bizarre" exhibit we've ever seen was..._____
_____

$$E = mc^2$$

TRANSPORTATION

KIDS AHEAD

Remove This Page

(to reduce binding thickness as you add personal photos)

Carefully cut along the dotted line

Use these cutouts
to add more fun to
your pages!

Outdoor Exploring

Learn the secret to protecting perfect beaches, forests and gardens. Climb a real lighthouse or hike across giant bridges. Hear the roar of huge, cascading falls or the gentle drips of stalactites, or the ech-o-o-o-o of a canyon. Splash water on fossil beds and make them "come alive" and walk on the top of a mountain across a natural bridge.

The effects of time and weather on natural formations are best seen at..._____

_____

Our favorite way to explore the outdoors...by car, van, sailboat, canoe, motorboat, bikes, etc..._____

_____

The State Park where we did the most ..._____

_____

Unforgettable finds in nature and animals that crossed our path..._____

_____

Our "hottest" beach spot..._____

_____

The most pretty and clean place we had a picnic..._____

_____

The best "fish story" we heard on our journeys..._____

_____

Wonderful waterfalls..._____

_____

Remove This Page

(to reduce binding thickness as you add personal photos)

Carefully
cut along
the dotted
line

Use these cutouts to add more fun to your pages!

Seasonal & Special Events

Eat your way through apple, cherry, barbecue, berry, cereal, ice cream (or even just ice), maple syrup, melon, popcorn and pumpkin festivals (wow...what a mouthful!). Drive through a Festival of Lights, take a train ride with Santa, watch the skies light up with a fireworks show, tramp through a pumpkin patch, or hop into an Easter egg hunt. Taste the cuisine and enjoy the dances of Germany, Scotland, Greece, Italy, Mexico, Poland, Ireland, Switzerland...to name just a few!

Our favorite fruit festival was..._____

_____

A holiday activity that has become a family tradition..._____

_____

Main Street celebrations - floats, parades, fireworks, and clowns that we saw were..._____

_____

_____

Our favorite ethnic festival and what we liked the best (besides the food!)..._____

_____

Our favorite ethnic foods..._____

_____

The first Native American "Pow-wow" that we experienced was ..._____

_____

Our favorite fair foods..._____

_____

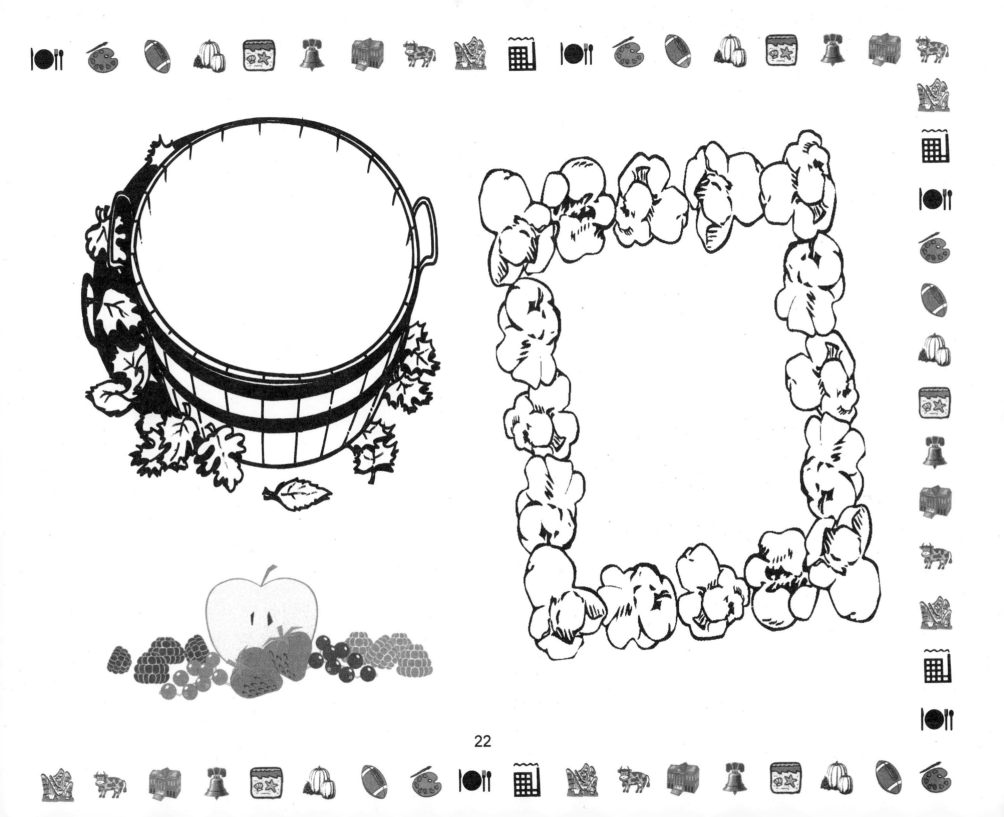

22

Remove This Page

(to reduce binding thickness as you add personal photos)

Carefully
cut along
the dotted
line

Use these cutouts to add more fun to your pages!

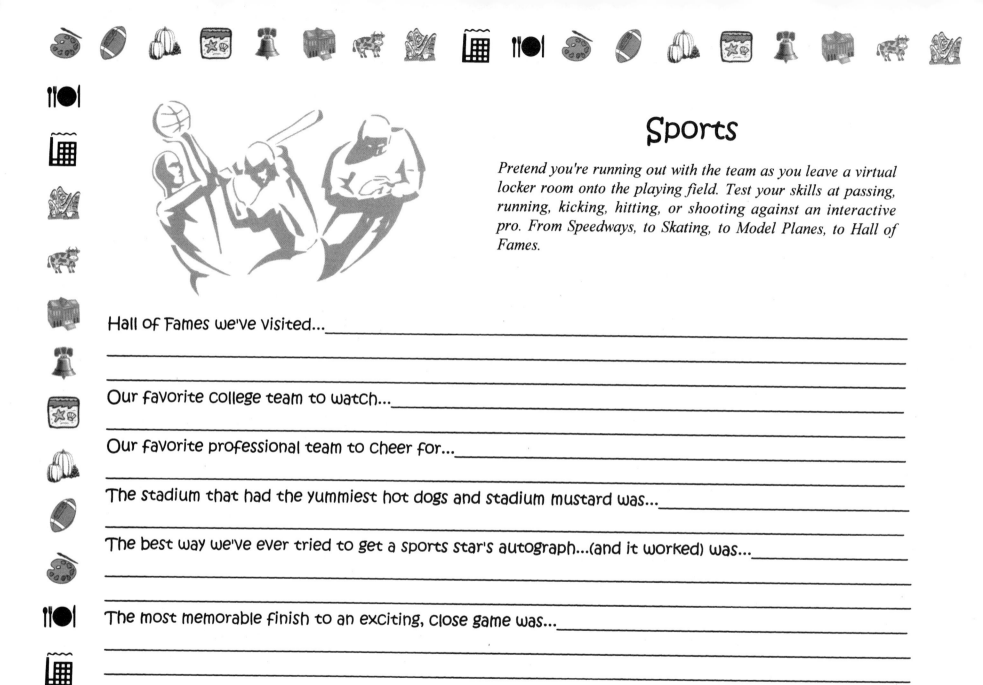

Sports

Pretend you're running out with the team as you leave a virtual locker room onto the playing field. Test your skills at passing, running, kicking, hitting, or shooting against an interactive pro. From Speedways, to Skating, to Model Planes, to Hall of Fames.

Hall of Fames we've visited..._____

_____

_____

Our favorite college team to watch..._____

_____

Our favorite professional team to cheer for..._____

_____

The stadium that had the yummiest hot dogs and stadium mustard was..._____

_____

The best way we've ever tried to get a sports star's autograph...(and it worked) was..._____

_____

_____

The most memorable finish to an exciting, close game was..._____

_____

_____

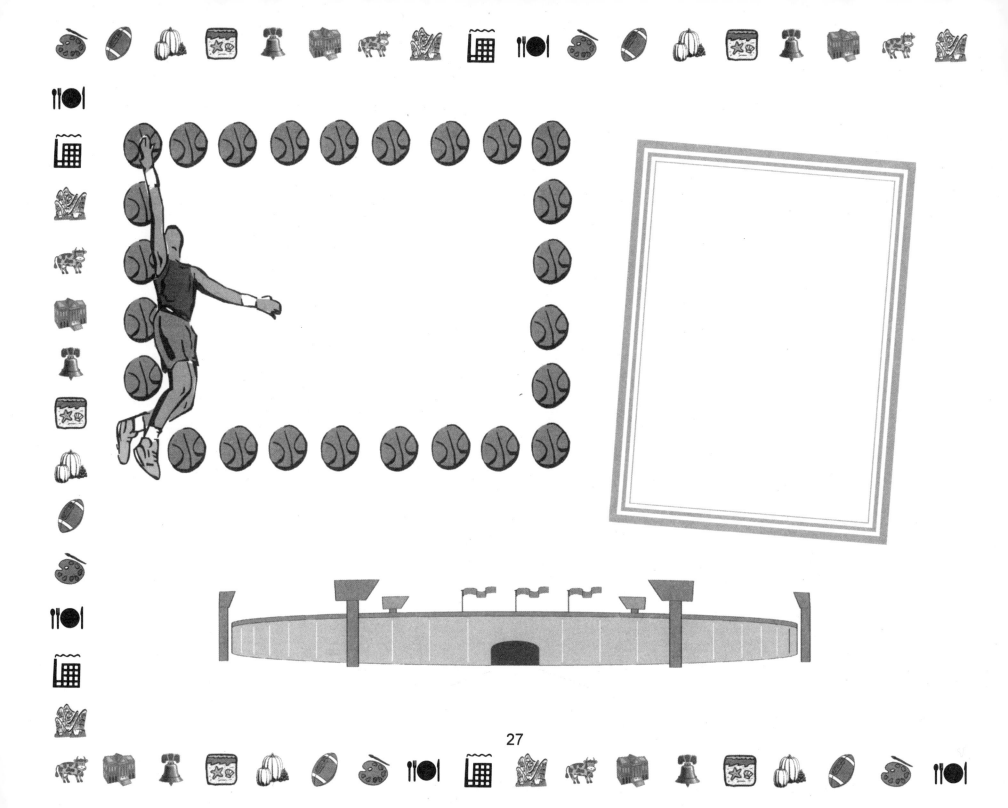

Remove This Page
(to reduce binding thickness as you add personal photos)

Carefully
cut along
the dotted
line

Use these cutouts to add more fun to your pages!

WINNING THE
RACE

The Arts

Discover all the things that can be called "art" from Old Toys & Garbage, to paintings over 6 stories tall! What is "Sgraffito"? - Not a famous artist...but a way a painting by scratching through layers of paint to get to the color you want! Re-live the trials and triumphs of famous legends like Daniel Boone, Abraham Lincoln, Jenny Wiley, Tecumseh, Jesus, Noah, and Stephen Foster (just to name a few) on stage.

The curtains up! Concerts (indoors or out), plays we saw and loved..._____
_____
_____

Our favorite character (s) in a play..._____
_____

Voted best art museum for kids..._____
_____

The most unique pieces of art we saw were..._____
_____

Artists or performers that we got to meet..._____
_____
_____

Our favorite pieces of art...(we wanted to bring them home!)..._____
_____
_____

29

Remove This Page

(to reduce binding thickness as you add personal photos)

Carefully
cut along
the dotted
line

Use these cutouts to add more fun to your pages!

Theme Restaurants

Taste foods called Burgoos, Cincinnati Chili, Gorilla Grilled Cheese Sandwiches, Hobo Sandwiches, Hot Browns, or Pasties. Imagine dining in an "elegant fast food" restaurant - (even one with a glass elevator!). Eat in a real one room schoolhouse, an old train depot, a real log cabin (maybe one Abe Lincoln dined at), a service station, a riverboat, a rainforest, a firehouse, or the famous 50's style diner!

Some specialities of the house - some "favorite items" that we'll come back for ... _____
_____
_____

Without a doubt this restaurant had the best kid's menu..._____
_____

Some new foods that the kids tried...and we never thought they'd eat..._____
_____
_____

The most unique restaurant environment..._____
_____
_____

The most historical place where we dined..._____
_____
_____

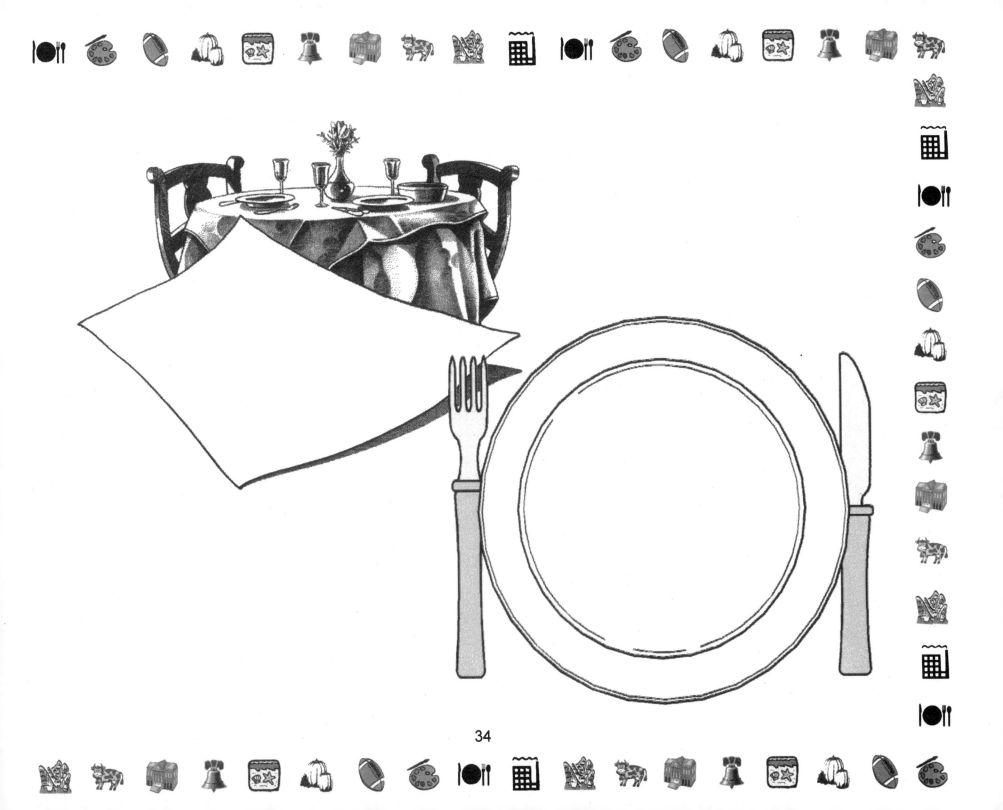

Remove This Page

(to reduce binding thickness as you add personal photos)

Carefully cut along the dotted line

Use these cutouts to add more fun to your pages!

PROUDLY

MADE IN THE USA

Tours

Learn how men made castles from stones or watch your favorite toys being made. If you're hungry, why not try your hand at making (or watch them make) candy, cereal, cheese, ice cream, pasta, pizza, popcorn, soda pop, potato chips, or be a pretzel twister. Stand side-by-side with a miner, a glass blower, a printer, a potter, a boat captain, a train conductor (maybe even on "Thomas the Tank Engine"). Watch a vehicle being assembled or see millions of U.S. coins being made before your eyes! Learn the secrets to perfect pottery and woven baskets or linens. Go behind the scenes of airports, banks, newspapers, post offices, supermarkets and TV & radio stations.

During our favorite tours, we watched this stuff being made..._____
_____
_____

This tour was the longest...but boy we sure learned a lot..._____
_____
_____

We got our favorite free souvenir at..._____
_____

The best kept secret or hidden tour was..._____
_____

The most "hands-on" tour was..._____
_____

Our top picks for transportation tours (boat, plane, train & bus)..._____
_____

CHIP

ICE CREAM

38

Remove This Page

(to reduce binding thickness as you add personal photos)

Carefully
cut along
the dotted
line

Use these cutouts to add more fun to your pages!

 Travel Thoughts...

 Our touring vehicle...(like one of the family was)..._____

_____

On <u>long trips</u> you really learn new things about your family..._____

_____

_____

_____

We made several new friends here..._____

_____

Our favorite place to be in the morning..._____

_____

Our favorite place to be in the evening..._____

_____

Tracking our trails, who's really the best at reading those maps..._____

_____

The trip with the most wrong turns..._____

_____

_____

_____

Remove This Page

(to reduce binding thickness as you add personal photos)

Carefully
cut along
the dotted
line

Use these cutouts to add more fun to your pages!

TRAVEL NOTES

GROUP DISCOUNTS & FUNDRAISING OPPORTUNITIES!

We're excited to introduce our books to your group! These guides for parents, grandparents, teachers and visitors are great tools to help you discover hundreds of fun places to visit. KIDS ♥ PUBLICATIONS titles are great resources for all the wonderful places to travel either locally or across the region. We are two parents who have researched, written and published these books. We have spent thousands of hours collecting information and <u>personally traveled over 10,000 miles</u> visiting all of the most unique places listed in our guides. The books are kid-tested and the descriptions include great hints on what kids like best!

"Kids Love Travel Memories" is the perfect companion to our best-selling family travel books. We suggest organizing a "scrapbooking" night within your group to have fun creating your family memory book!

Please consider the following Group Purchase options: For the latest information, visit our website: **www.kidslovepublications.com**

- ❑ **Group Discount/Fundraising** – Purchase books at the price of ($10.00 - $11.00 each) and offer the (~25+%) savings off the suggested retail price to members/friends. <u>Minimum order is 10 books for group purchase</u>. You may mix titles to reach the minimum order. Greater discounts (~35%) are available for fundraisers. Call for details. (<u>Minimum order is 30 books for fund-raisers</u>)
- ❑ **Available for Interview/Speaking** – The authors have a treasure bag full of souvenirs from favorite places. We'd love to share ideas on planning fun trips to take children while exploring your home state. The authors are available, by appointment, at (614) 792-6451. The minimum guaranteed order is: 30 books in Ohio, 50 books for other states. There is no additional fee involved.

Call us soon at (614) 792-6451 to make arrangements! - *Happy Exploring!*

ORDER FORM

KIDS LOVE PUBLICATIONS

7438 Sawmill Road, # 500
Columbus, OH 43235
(614) 792-6451
Visit our website: **www.kidslovepublications.com**

#	Title		Price	Total
	Kids Love Indiana		$12.95	
	Kids Love Michigan		$12.95	
	Kids Love Pennsylvania		$12.95	
	Kids Love Ohio		$13.95	
	Kids Love Kentucky		$13.95	
	Kids Love Travel Memories		$14.95	
Special Combo Pricing – Please Indicate Quantity & Titles Above				
	Combo #2 - Any 2 Titles		$22.95	
	Combo #3 - Any 3 Titles		$31.95	
	Combo #4 - Any 4 Titles		$39.95	

Note: All combo pricing is for different titles only . For multiple copies (10+) <u>of one</u> title, please call or visit our website for volume discounts.		**Subtotal**	
	(Ohio Residents Only) $1.00 per book	Sales Tax	
		Shipping	
		TOTAL	

[] Master Card [] Visa

Account Number _ _ _ _ - _ _ _ _ - _ _ _ _ - _ _ _ _
Exp Date: _ _ / _ _ (Month/Year)
Cardholder's Name _____
Signature *(required)* _____

(Please make check or money order payable to: KIDS LOVE PUBLICATIONS)

Name: _____
Address:_____
City:_____ State:_____
Zip:_____ Telephone:_____

All orders are shipped within 2 business days of receipt by US Mail or Fed-X Ground. Your satisfaction is 100% guaranteed or simply return your order for a prompt refund. Thanks for your order!

Attention Parents:

All titles are "Kid Tested". *The authors and kids personally visited all of the most unique places* and wrote the books with warmth and excitement from a parent's perspective. Find tried and true places that children will enjoy. No more boring trips! Listings provide: Names, addresses, telephone numbers, <u>websites</u> (*except Kids Love Indiana*), directions, and descriptions. All books include a <u>bonus chapter</u> listing state-wide kid-friendly Seasonal & Special Events!

KIDS LOVE INDIANA ™

❖ **Discover places where you can "co-star" in a cartoon or climb a giant sand dune.** Almost 600 listings in one book about Indiana travel. 10 geographical zones, 193 pages.

KIDS LOVE KENTUCKY ™

❖ **Discover places from Boone to Burgoo, from Caves to Corvettes, and from Lincoln to the Lands of Horses.** Over 500 listings in one book about Kentucky travel. 6 geographic zones. 224 pages.

KIDS LOVE MICHIGAN ™

❖ **Discover places where you can "race" over giant sand dunes, climb aboard a lighthouse "ship", eat at the world's largest breakfast table, or watch yummy foods being made.** Almost 600 listings in one book about Michigan travel. 8 geographical zones, 237 pages.

KIDS LOVE OHIO ™

❖ **Discover places like hidden castles and whistle factories.** Almost 1000 listings in one book about Ohio travel. 9 geographical zones, 257 pages.

KIDS LOVE PENNSYLVANIA ™

❖ **Explore places where you can "discover" oil and coal, meet Ben Franklin, or watch you favorite toys and delicious, fresh snacks being made.** Over 900 listings in one book about Pennsylvania travel. 9 geographical zones, 268 pages.

KIDS LOVE TRAVEL MEMORIES ™

The perfect travel journal & scrapbook companion to our books!